SUPER HAPPY PARTY BEARS

GNAWING

AROUND

GNAWING AROUND

MARCIE COLLEEN

[imprint]
MAKE YOUR MARK

NEW YORK

{Imprint}
MAKE YOUR MARK

A part of Macmillan Children's Publishing Group,
a division of Macmillan Publishing Group, LLC

SUPER HAPPY PARTY BEARS: GNAWING AROUND. Copyright © 2016 by Imprint.
All rights reserved. Printed in China by Toppan Leefung Printing Ltd.,
Dongguan City, Guangdong Province. For information,
address Imprint, 175 Fifth Avenue, New York, N.Y. 10010.

Library of Congress Cataloging-in-Publication Data is available.
ISBN 978-1-250-13117-1
Our books may be purchased in bulk for promotional, educational,
or business use. Please contact your local bookseller or the Macmillan
Corporate and Premium Sales Department at (800) 221-7945 ext. 5442
or by e-mail at MacmillanSpecialMarkets@macmillan.com.

Book design by Natalie C. Sousa
Imprint logo designed by Amanda Spielman
Illustrations by Steve James

First Edition—2016

1 3 5 7 9 10 8 6 4 2

mackids.com

If this book isn't yours, keep your thieving paws off it. Obey or may the
elastic string on all of your party hats snap before you even get them on.

TO THE THREE E'S WITH LOVE

CHAPTER ONE

Welcome to the Grumpy Woods!

Just kidding. No one is welcome here. Turn around and go back. The Grumpy Woods doesn't need any new residents—and it especially doesn't need any more bears. Especially not bears who

like to dance and sing and make
doughnuts and have parties. If you
are a bear, then *stay out.*

Of course, right now you might
be thinking, *Bears are cute* and
Parties are fun. Cut it out. The
animals of the Grumpy Woods do

not agree, because everyone here

who's not a bear is, well, *grumpy*.

So don't bother looking for a

welcome sign, because it's been

taken down. All welcome mats

and mailboxes have also been

removed. That's right. They were

all taken down by an official
decree of the mayor.

Mayor Quill had an official
meeting at City Hall. (City Hall is
really just an upturned log, not

actually a hall of any sort, but
don't tell Mayor Quill that. He
takes his position quite seriously.)

The Super Happy Party Bears
were not invited to the meeting.

At that meeting, everyone—
from Bernice Bunny to Humphrey
Hedgehog—decided that *no one*
was welcome in the Grumpy Woods

and that anything welcoming
should be removed.

They voted. And that was that.
It was very official.

And so, every day, everyone in
the Grumpy Woods wakes up on
the wrong side of the bed, puts on
their cranky pants (actually, more
like a whole outfit), and orders

up some breakfast—two scoops
of crabby in a bowlful of *Leave me
alone!* That is, everyone except the
Super Happy Party Bears.

Over at the Party Patch, the
Headquarters of Fun—where the
Super Happy Party Bears have made
their home—life is very different.

LIFE IS SUPER. Life

is happy. And life is full of parties!

Remember the mailboxes and

the welcome mats? They were

mentioned about seven paragraphs

ago. Well, you will find that

they have been relocated

to the Party Patch. The

mailboxes dangle like ornaments from the shrubbery. The welcome mats are stacked like a house of cards to create a cozy canopy in front of the main entrance. The main entrance is easy to find because carefully placed sticks, laid out in the shape

of arrows, lead any would-be
visitor up a flower-lined path,
straight to the Super Happy
Party Bears' den.

Oh, and that welcome sign?
Well, that can be found at the
Party Patch, too. On top of
the sign sits a little stick-figure
diorama that includes the likeness
of a few Grumpy Woods neighbors.

They are wearing party hats and dancing. The leader of the party appears to be Mayor Quill.

See, while the others in the Grumpy Woods can't stand the bears, the Super Happy Party Bears *adore* their neighbors, especially Mayor Quill.

And so, on a beautiful morning such as this, the Super Happy Party Bears get up on the cheeriest side of the bed, put on their pants of positivity, and order up some breakfast—two triple-decker giggle-and-jelly sandwiches and a bowlful of *The best day ever!*

Nothing annoys the critters of the Grumpy Woods more.

Except when the bears have a party.

And they are always having a

PARTY.

13

CHAPTER TWO

Mayor Quill was on some very important official business.

Angrily clutching a stack of envelopes in his paw, he stomped up the path marked with twig arrows and lined with cheerful flowers. Signs along the way pointed to the Party Patch. Sounds of celebration were coming out of the shrubs up ahead—it sounded like the song "If You're Happy and You Know It," complete with a pots-and-pans rhythm section. It sounded like a party—a *breakfast party.*

And then he was in front of it—
the welcome sign.

Mayor Quill squinted at the tiny
Mayor Quill stick figure dancing
atop the wooden sign, and his
quills bristled.

"That tiny party hat makes
me look fat," he mumbled, and
bumped into the sign on purpose
as he waddled by, hoping to topple
it. But to his dismay, the mayor
stick figure simply tipped into the
other stick neighbors in a kind of
group hug.

"BAH!" griped Mayor Quill as
he crumpled the letters in his paw.

For a week now, Mayor Quill
had been getting these letters.
He kept finding them all over

City Hall. With no mailbox for his mail, Mayor Quill was finding letters under his pillow, inside his morning bowl of leaves and berries, and even in his underwear drawer! And they all said the most annoying things:

You're Swell.

Who's the best mayor around? You are!

Way 2 Go!

The cheery letters had the paw prints of the Super Happy Party

Bears all over them, and Mayor
Quill was fed up.

He started to cram the letters
under the door. The breakfast bash
abruptly stopped, and the mayor
heard the shuffle of a dozen pairs of
furry feet gather on the other side.
"ONE! TWO! THREE! WHO CAN
IT BEEEEEEEEEE?" sang the bears,
before swinging the door open wide.

19

"QUILLY!" they all cheered.

Mayor Quill threw up his hands in surprise, and the envelopes flew into the air.

"He's delivering *mail* to us," said the littlest bear as he gathered up the wrinkled envelopes.

And before Mayor Quill could object, he was pulled into the

Party Patch and a cup of juice put
in his paw.

"I'm actually here on very
important official business
regarding this mail," said Mayor
Quill.

"This is the most special morning
ever!" cheered the bears. "It's
official! This calls for another party!

"IT'S SUPER HAPPY PARTY
TIME! SUPER HAPPY PARTY TIME!"
the bears chanted, and they did
their Super Happy Party Dance.

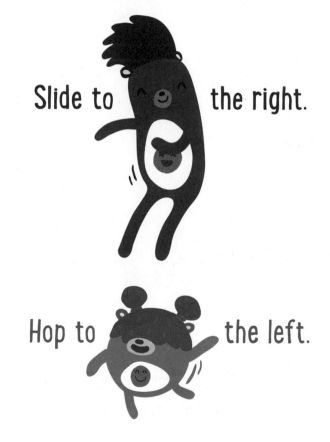

Slide to the right.

Hop to the left.

Shimmy, shimmy, shake.

Strike a pose.

"We must provide refreshments for this party!" announced a small bear, breaking his dance pose. It was Mops, named for his mop-top hair that fell over his eyes.

"This isn't a party," said Mayor
Quill. "More like a meeting."

"A meeting is just a party
without doughnuts," said Bubs
as he calmly blew party-perfect
bubbles. Bubs was always the
voice of party wisdom.

"DOUGHNUTS!" they all cheered,
and scrambled off in a flurry.

Pans clattered and batter

splattered everywhere as the

bears busied themselves preparing the doughnuts. Meanwhile, the littlest bear delivered the mail.

"'You're swell.' This one must be for you." He handed the letter to Shades, who winked over his star glasses. And to a bear who was doing jumping jacks he said,

"'Way 2 Go!' is definitely meant for you, Jacks."

The littlest bear then hesitated.
"'Who's the best mayor around?'
Silly, Quilly! That's YOU!"

"These letters were—" the
mayor protested.

"—meant to make us happy?"
asked the bears sweetly. "THEY
DID!"

Just then, Mayor Quill felt a
tug on one of his back quills.
He turned around to see a bear
wearing some sort of armor made
out of twigs and pinecones.

"What in the world are you wearing?" he asked.

"It's the newly patented Hug-a-Mayor suit. It allows us to hug a porcupine such as yourself repeatedly, and for longer periods, without getting poked."

The mayor backed away awkwardly from the outstretched padded arms. There was nothing Mayor Quill hated more than hugs. Except for maybe stumbling backward and sitting right in a big bowl of doughnut batter.

He didn't want hugs, or

doughnuts, or mail, or a party.

The mayor just wanted a bath.

CHAPTER THREE

Mayor Quill plucked a fresh sharp quill from his backside and flicked off a bit of batter before dipping the quill into his inkpot. He carefully added to the Mayoral Decree he had hung on the tallest tree at the center of the woods. It was basically

a list of rules to follow—but the
porcupine liked the sound of the
word *decree*. It was very official.

He underlined the words *DOES*
and *NOT*—not once, not twice,

but five times. He was not messing around.

He stepped back to examine his work and shook his rump a little, trying to shake off the goopy mess. It was time for a long, hot bath.

Mayor Quill hung his **CLOSED FOR OFFICIAL BUSINESS** sign on his door and then stepped

inside the official City Hall—which was really just the log he lived in—and went to his private, members-only watering hole, of which he was the only member. He cued up the whirlpool for his bubble bath.

Of course, the whirlpool was really just Arlo Rabbit, kicker extraordinaire, who could strike up a current in the calmest of

waters with his hind legs and who
didn't mind the exercise. Arlo was
good about covering his eyes to
give Mayor Quill privacy.

But when the mayor stepped into the tub he had made by carving a knot out of the log, the water level seemed incredibly low.

"That's odd," he muttered. "You have your work cut out for you today, Arlo."

Just then there was a knock at the trunk.

Mayor Quill wanted nothing more than to soak in the tub, rid his tush of doughnut batter, and get on with his day. He ignored the knock.

Knock, knocky, knock-knock.

Mayor Quill would know that pestering knock anywhere. He wanted to disappear deeper into the water—but the water barely covered his rump.

The door opened a crack.

"Mayor Quill, sir?" It was Humphrey Hedgehog.

"What do you want?" the mayor barked. "I'm in the bath."

"I figured as much, sir."

Humphrey Hedgehog was the mayor's assistant deputy. By

now he had entered the private,
members-only watering hole.
Nothing bugged the mayor more
than when Humphrey considered
himself an equal.

37

"I'm covering my eyes, sir. I won't see a thing. I just wanted to let you know there seems to be a problem with the water. It is missing, sir."

"You don't say?" responded Mayor Quill.

"Yes, sir. Indeed. Someone must have stolen it. And I have a list

of possible culprits that I would
like you to review at your earliest
convenience." Humphrey flipped
through at least ten pages
on his clipboard.

Out of the corner
of his eye, the mayor
caught a glimpse of the
top of Humphrey's list.

possible culprits
1. The Super
    Happy
    Party Bears
2. Thirsty Birds

The mayor looked down at his shallow bathwater. Some chunks of doughnut floated by, and rainbow sprinkles bobbed on the surface.

Squirrelly Sam suddenly appeared, scrambling down from the branches above to hang his head upside down in the doorway, completely ignoring the sign out front.

"Excuse me, Mr. Mayor. I have a mail delivery for you."

Mayor Quill stomped his foot. He shook from head to toe. Just before the mayor exploded, Humphrey rolled into a defensive ball. Being a hedgehog, he had his own spiny exterior. It came in handy at times like these.

Quills exploded everywhere. One narrowly missed Arlo's ear. Another speared the mail, tearing it out of Sam's paw and pinning it to a tree several feet away.

Humphrey peeked out from behind his clipboard.

"Good shot, sir."

CHAPTER FOUR

Mayor Quill never got his bath.
Soon City Hall was crawling with
complainers about the water
situation. No, really. Folks *actually*
climbed onto the rotten upturned
log and demanded a town meeting.

As Mayor Quill prepared to

address his people, Humphrey made preparations of his own.

"Excuse me, Humphrey," said Sam as he skittered in circles around Humphrey's short legs. Nothing made Squirrelly Sam squirrellier than when he had a big juicy piece of gossip to share. "You didn't hear this from me, but . . ."

Humphrey didn't hear it at all.
Nothing could distract the assistant
deputy. He was busy practicing the
speech he would give to the Super
Happy Party Bears.

"It has come to City Hall's
attention," muttered Humphrey,
"that you have stolen our water.
Your shenanigans have gone on

far too long, and it is upon order of the mayor himself that I must ask you to relocate." Humphrey chuckled to himself. This was a moment he had dreamed of often. And this was a speech he had rehearsed every night in his dreams, too. Getting rid of the Super Happy Party Bears would

surely make him a hero in the
Grumpy Woods. And heroes can
become mayors.

By now Sam was on top of
Humphrey's head, struggling to
make eye contact upside down.

" . . . gnashing and gnawing with
their ginormous teeth. Are you
listening, Humphrey?"

It was evident by Humphrey's glazed-over eyes that he was not listening to Sam's story but was instead daydreaming of his mayoral inauguration party.

Sam sighed exasperatedly and began all over again.

Humphrey fought to half listen, catching bits and pieces—

"... newcomers ... all night long ... TIIIIIMBERRRRR!"—until Mayor

Quill took the podium, signaling
the beginning of the town meeting.

But before the mayor even
finished clearing his throat, a
voice rang out from the crowd.
"My beautiful Grumpy River.
Someone stole it! Now I will never
finish my book!" cried out Bernice
Bunny.

Bernice was known to sit for hours on the banks of the Grumpy River with her twitchy nose stuck in a book.

Everyone in Grumpy Woods knew to tiptoe by quietly. Bernice hated to be interrupted. Rumor had it that she'd been reading the same book for five years because the Super Happy Party Bears disturbed her so many times she had to keep reading the same paragraph over and over and over.

Frantic murmurs bubbled up from the gathered bunch.

"Stolen?"

"Gone?"

"The *whole* river?"

"Makes sense," said Mayor
Quill. "I once heard the Super
Happy Party Bears planning a pool
party. But they don't have a pool!"

The group gasped.

Humphrey worked out his own
prediction. "I know they were
making doughnuts this morning.

Large quantities of sugary doughnuts can make one awfully thirsty. All they would need is a giant straw and *slurp!* The water would be all sucked up."

"Well, you didn't hear it from me, but—" started Squirrelly Sam. And he was right. No one heard him. They were all too busy talking over one another, accusing the Super Happy Party Bears of ruining the river.

"Please! Everybody! One at a time," yelled Mayor Quill as he banged his gavel on the podium.

"All night I tossed and turned to the terrible sound of crunching and chewing!"

"There are mountains of sawdust where trees once stood!"

"Dirty, dirty, dirty. Too much to clean," sang Dawn Fawn, who sang whenever she felt nervous. She really liked to keep things clean. Sometimes she even used Bernice's tail as a dust mop.

"Obviously, they are making lounge chairs for their pool party," stated Bernice matter-of-factly as she slowly stepped away from Dawn.

"Or they are making Popsicles

again," said Humphrey, "and need more sticks."

Sam excitedly continued his previous tale. By now he was so out of breath he was only speaking in fragments. "It's the monsters. Draining water. Obliterating trees. All night long. TIIIIIMMMBBBEEEEERRRRR!"

"There are no monsters in the Grumpy Woods," interrupted Mayor Quill, who was finally listening to Sam.

"I wouldn't be too ssssure of that," came a hiss from the ground. It was Sherry Snake, self-proclaimed sheriff of the Grumpy Woods. Sherry made it her duty

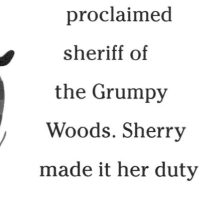

to secure and protect the borders of the Grumpy Woods. Mostly, she just enjoyed telling other animals to scram.

"M-m-m-monsters?" Bernice's fuzzy ears trembled.

"Really, Sherry, this isn't helping," harrumphed Humphrey.

"I told them to sssstay out," continued Sherry, "but they ssssaid sssssnakessssskin was so lasssst ssssspring and laughed at me."

"This doesn't make sense," said Mayor Quill.

"Exactly. Sssssnakesssskin is alwaysss in sssseasssson."

"I'll tell you what doesn't make sense," echoed a voice from the back. It was Opal Owl, pulling a curler out of her feathers and plucking bits of her nest from her waist. "It is morning and I am awake! I thought we all gave a hoot about peace and quiet."

"Our deepest apologies, Opal," said Mayor Quill. But before he could promise to keep the noise level down, the ground rumbled. The leaves rustled.

"It can't be," mumbled the mayor.

The Grumpy Woods neighbors' greatest fear was rolling by City Hall.

The welcome wagon.

Covered with welcome banners,
signs, and pennants, it was packed
with everything a good neighbor
needs to greet newcomers:
casseroles, cups of sugar to
borrow, fruit baskets, and muffins.

61

There was even a red carpet tied to the front, ready to be rolled out.

The wagon was being pulled along by the Super Happy Party Bears.

"There will be no welcoming in the Woods as stated by Mayoral Decree one-point-three-A!" Humphrey called after the wagon.

"Sssstop them!" hissed Sherry.

And all the townscritters
got in line after the bears
and headed down to the river.
When the Super Happy Party
Bears realized they were being
followed, they cheered.
"WE LOVE PARADES!" they
shouted, and marched that
sourpuss of a procession straight
to the monsters.

CHAPTER FIVE

There on the banks of the Grumpy

River was not a pair of monsters

but a pair of beavers. Next to the

pair of beavers was a heap of

sticks, logs, trunks, and twigs of

all shapes and sizes. The wood

was twisted and woven together

to create a mound that stretched
across the river and held back the
flow of water. Upriver the water
bulged and swelled. Yet downriver
it was barely a trickle.

The beavers hoisted more trees,
one by one, onto the pile.

"Truly magnificent," said one
beaver.

"Absolutely. The best river views in all of real estate," replied the other beaver.

"Nothing but the best for my Mitzi-witzy," responded the first beaver.

The Grumpy Woods residents stayed back, their mouths hanging open. But then the Super Happy Party Bears sprang into action.

"WELCOME TO THE GRUMPY
WOODS!" they cheered, and rolled
out the red carpet—literally.

"Oh dear," said the beaver
named Mitzi, obviously startled.
"Nelson, I thought you said this
was a *secluded* area."

"Why, yes, Mitzi darling.
Apparently these *bears* are a bit

lost." And then under his breath to the bears, Nelson said, "Get lost."

"We're not lost," said Mops. "We're your neighbors!"

At the word *neighbors*, Mitzi practically fainted.

Three more beavers suddenly

poked their heads out from the pile of trees and leaves in the middle of the river. "What's all the commotion?" they asked. "It woke the baby."

"Oh, nothing, Devon. Nothing to worry about, Cricket. Just some riffraff passing by."

"We brought a casserole," said the littlest bear.

Nelson approached, sniffed the casserole, and then passed it off to Devon. "This might work to seal up that crack in the foundation."

Meanwhile, Cricket and Mitzi inspected the red carpet for possible use in their beaver lodge perched on top of the dam.

"Very well," said Nelson. "Now, if you don't mind, we are on a bit of a schedule."

"But we haven't played our icebreaker name game yet," said Jacks. "You go first, Nelson, so we

can learn your name."

"My name is Nelson."

"No. Say something like, 'My name is Nelson, and I'm bringing noodles to the party.'"

"I am *not* bringing any noodles."

"Nuts?"

"No."

"Napkins?"

"Nope."

"You have to bring something,
Nelson," explained Shades. "So
that we learn your name."

"My name is Nelson, and
apparently I'm bringing
nincompoops to the party."

"HELLO, NELSON!" cheered the
bears.

"HUG TIME!"

Nelson, however, was saved as Mayor Quill stepped forward.

"Allow me to introduce *my*self," he said. "I am Quill, mayor of the Grumpy Woods."

The littlest bear pouted. "Quilly, you aren't playing correctly! You always say, 'My name is Mayor

Quill, and I am bringing *quiet* to the party.' Silly Quilly!"

"Listen, I do appreciate this little shindig or whatever," said Nelson, "but I really must be getting back to work. Dams don't build themselves, you know."

"Can we have a tour when it's finished?" asked Mops.

"Certainly," said Nelson sarcastically. "I can think of nothing more thrilling. In fact, let's sell tickets."

Mayor Quill chuckled. "Hee-hee. Silly bears." He winked at Nelson to prove he understood how annoying the bears were. "No one is taking any tours. Now, if we could all just give the beavers some space, they can pack up and move on."

Nelson chuckled. "Hee-hee. Silly mayor. No one is packing up and moving on. Now, if you all could kindly get off my property . . ."

"*Your* property?" fumed Mayor Quill. "This is the Grumpy Woods!"

"Ah yes. And so I say, quite *grumpily*, YOU ARE NOT WELCOME HERE!" announced Nelson. And he waddled off, using his big flat tail to slam the door of the lodge behind him.

CHAPTER SIX

Between the quill storms and the many decrees he had written, the mayor was going to be bald by dinnertime.

"'Mayoral Decree two hundred thirty-eight,'" Mayor Quill read aloud as he wrote. "'Beavers are a nuisance and should be treated as such.'"

"Well said, sir," said Humphrey. "How dare they speak to you like that!"

"Ssssomething sssshould be done," said Sherry.

"We should write them a letter," suggested Bernice Bunny.

"No more mail," groaned
Mayor Quill, still reeling from his
morning visit to the Party Patch.
He continued writing. "'Mayoral
Decree two hundred thirty-nine:
The welcome wagon shall be rolled
off Grumpy Cliff immediately.'"

"Whoooomever heard of a
welcome wagon?" scoffed Opal.

"We will *un*welcome that wagon.
Smash! Crash!" added Bernice.

"I can think of a few other things
I'd like to roll off Grumpy Cliff,"
mumbled Humphrey.

"That's it!" said Mayor Quill.
"Let's *un*welcome the beavers!"

"You want to roll them off the
cliff?" asked Dawn.

81

"No, no," answered Quill. "I suggest we make an *un*welcome sign."

Humphrey waggled his spines. "Most excellent, sir. Once the beavers realize they are unwelcome, they will surely move on!"

Everyone grumbled about it, but no one had a better idea, so they got to work.

Sam's bushy tail made the perfect scary brushstrokes when dipped in berry juice. Dawn Fawn provided a pile of burrs collected during her most recent sweeping of the Woods. And when Sheriff Sherry set her mind to it, her fangs did some amazing whittling.

When they were done, the sign
was drippy. It was spiky. And it
was *un*welcoming.

To show their solidarity, the
townscritters took the sign to the
river shore by the beavers' dam.
Together, they smacked it into the
ground.

As they proudly marched away,

Mayor Quill glanced back and was sure he could see four pairs of beady eyes peering out from the lodge. He was certain it would be only a matter of time until the beavers packed their things and left to clog up someone else's river someplace far away.

And maybe that would have happened . . . if the Super Happy

Party Bears hadn't gone to the riverbank, too, just after them.

"What a beautiful sign," they squealed. After all, it was prickly and reminded them of their beloved mayor. "What a wonderful idea!"

"'Unwelcome to the Grumpy Woods,'" read Mops. "What do you suppose that means?"

"It's actually 'UN Welcome to the Grumpy Woods,'" explained

Bubbles, briefly pausing his bubble blowing. "There's a space. It stands for *United Neighbors Welcome to the Grumpy Woods*."

"YAY! We LOVE the United Neighbors!" cheered the bears. "We should go to their next meeting."

"And bring doughnuts," added the littlest bear.

"Kindly get off our lawn!" came a voice from inside the lodge.

"NELSON!" cheered the bears.

"We came to retrieve our casserole dish," said Shades. "No worries if you didn't have time to wash it and fill it up with something equally tasty. We understand that moving can be stressful."

"What's that sign?" asked Nelson.

"On behalf of the United Neighbors," proclaimed Mops, "we

welcome you, once again, to the Grumpy Woods."

The bears did a dance.

Slide to the right.

Hop to the left.

Shimmy, shimmy, shake.

Strike a pose.

CHAPTER SEVEN

The four beavers came outside
and stood gazing up at the ghastly
sign. The baby beaver cried.

"It's quite tacky, isn't it?"
whispered Devon.

"Truly," agreed Mitzi as quietly
as her rising blood pressure would

allow. "Next thing you know, these bears will be bringing us a pink plastic flamingo."

"Isn't it beautiful?" gushed the bears.

"Not quite the word I would choose," muttered Cricket.

"It makes mine look so teeny," said the littlest bear. He held up

a sign with a bow around its post

and a tag that read:

To: my favoritest neighbors

From: littlest bear

Painted on the sign were a

garden gnome and the words

"Oh, puns. How quaint," said

Mitzi, rolling her eyes.

"Puns are a sign of language mastery," stated Bubs.

"But the United Neighbors sign is so much more beautiful," said littlest bear, holding back tears.

Just then Nelson had an idea.

"Well, it seems to me that *United Neighbors* means that this sign could be placed *anywhere* in the woods. It's for *all* of us. While the gnome sign is a very special gift."

Cricket caught on quickly. "Oh yes. This humongous sign belongs where *others* can enjoy it."

"It would be a *crime* to keep it to ourselves," added Devon.

"We LOVE sharing!" cheered the bears. "Just wait until Quilly sees

this beautiful sign in front of City

Hall, where everyone can enjoy it!"

And that was that. The sign

went to City Hall. And the beavers

stayed.

As for the GNOME, SWEET GNOME

sign? Well, let's just say that the

beavers got a new doormat.

"Unwelcoming *us*?" said Mayor

Quill when he found the sign the next day. "The nerve of those beavers!"

"If they won't leave," said Humphrey, "then we will have to find a way to keep them out. Here's my new idea to unwelcome them: We will build a wall." He unrolled blueprints for a giant wall along the riverbank. "Sherry

can patrol from the ground. Sam will be able to spy from the tree branches above," he explained.

Everyone liked the idea. But no one cheered. They were too grumpy for that.

Instead, they got to work constructing the tallest, most towering wall ever.

Sam and Bernice were on saw— or gnaw—duty.

Opal flew high to hold the logs in place as Humphrey hammered them together using quills. (Don't ask where he got those from.)

Mayor Quill shouted orders. No surprise there.

And Dawn, of course, was on cleanup duty.

It was quite a team effort. The wall was twenty-four Sherrys long and eight Sherrys tall. Sherry had objected to being used as a ruler, but since they had no proper measuring instruments, she was forced to cooperate. When the wall was finished, the townscritters weren't the only ones applauding.

"A gated community! How wonderful," gushed Mitzi, a tear in her eye.

"Absolutely dreamy!" exclaimed Cricket.

Devon chuckled. "Seems we've seen the last of the riffraff."

"Good riddance," said Nelson.

But they had spoken too soon.

"A howdy and a half, neighbors!"

It was the bears. Apparently, twenty-four Sherrys long was not long enough. The bears simply walked around the wall.

"My, what persistent little legs you have, to go so long out of your

way to see us," said Mitzi, smiling
with clenched teeth.

"A wall between neighbors is
never long," stated Bubbles, who
then blew a huge, shiny bubble
that popped right on Nelson's
nose. POP!

The Super Happy Party
Bears loved visiting their new

neighbors—which really meant standing near the beavers, oohing and aahing over everything the beavers said, and occasionally breaking into a dance. The beavers had long ago decided that the only way to handle this kind of visit was to "not look them in the eye and hope they go away." So far it hadn't worked.

Over tea, the beavers were discussing the almost-finished lodge made of logs and leaves and sticks. They ignored the bears.

"Oh, how I wish we could create that sunroom," Mitzi said with a sigh. "It would be the absolute perfect spot where you could work

on the Sunday crossword puzzle,
Nelson."

"Indeed," agreed Cricket. "And
imagine the stargazing we could
do at night, Devon."

Although Devon and Nelson
wished to add a sunroom to
the lodge, there was
one very big issue.

106

"Unfortunately," said Nelson, "we are running out of logs."

"It's a pity there just isn't enough lumber." Devon sighed.

At that, the Super Happy Party Bears, excited to be of help, chimed in. "We know where there is plenty more wood!"

You see, there was a big flaw in the townscritters' plan. The only building material available in the Grumpy Woods was . . . well, wood.

And beavers chew wood and use it to build things. You can imagine what happened to the massive wooden fence—go ahead and imagine it.

There was a lot of chewing and gnawing, and by the next morning, Nelson, Devon, Mitzi, and Cricket had the sunroom they'd always wanted.

CHAPTER EIGHT

The Grumpy Woods was becoming the Even Grumpier Woods.

The unwelcome sign had disappeared. The gigantic fence had disappeared. The beavers had *not* disappeared, and they didn't seem to have any plans to do so.

Instead, the dam and the lodge
on top got bigger—just like the
townscritters' tempers.

"We need to come up with
another plan, sir," said Humphrey.

"Do you think I don't know
that?" Mayor Quill snapped.
Humphrey noticed the mayor's
quills beginning to tremble and
feared another quill storm.

110

"Whoever thought that ssssilly wall would work, anyhow?" complained Sherry.

"Who are you calling s-s-s-silly?" snapped Humphrey.

"Could you-hooooo keep it down? Some of us were ruuuudely awoken," hooted Opal.

"You didn't hear this from me, but . . ." started Sam.

111

"NOT NOW!" everyone shouted.

"It's hopeless! I NEED MY DUST BUNNY!" sang Dawn. The destruction of the wall had left behind piles of sawdust that Dawn was frantically trying to sweep up.

"Ack! No you don't!" protested Bernice. Bernice hated being used as Dawn's duster even more than

she hated being interrupted while reading.

"MUST CLEAN!

MUST DUST, MUST DUST, MUST
DUST!" Dawn sang out.

"QUIET!" yelled Mayor Quill.
"The last thing anyone wants to
hear right now is your singing.

If you don't stop, *I'm* going to leave the Grumpy Woods!"

"Sir, that's it, sir!" said Humphrey, perking up. "I have a plan! What's worse than Dawn's singing?"

No one had an answer.

"You, sir. *You* singing!"

"I beg your pardon," said Mayor Quill.

"Not *just* you, sir. All of us."

"Speak for yourself," hooted Opal.

"All right, maybe not Opal. But no one ever said, *Just listen to the beautiful sounds of that porcupine. Or hedgehog! Or squirrel!* If we become the Grumpy Woods Chorus, we can serenade those

 lumberjacks until they can't take it anymore!"

"My aunt Marty always did complain about my singing," admitted Sam.

"Rabbits are known to be unable to carry a tune. I read that in a book," said Bernice.

So off the townscritters went, looking like holiday carolers with attitude.

When they got to the lodge, they found the bears already

there, throwing a housewarming
party for their new neighbors.

"Look!" said the littlest bear.
"Everyone else came to the party,

too!" He clapped his paws in delight.

"SUPER HAPPY NEW HOME!" cheered the bears. "Let the housewarming party begin!"

"Hand out the doughnuts," added Mops.

Slide to the right.

 Hop to the left.

Shimmy, shimmy, shake.

Strike a pose.

119

The sun was starting to set,
and the beavers were indeed
celebrating the completion of their
new home . . . while doing their
best to ignore the other animals
around them.

"Simply lovely," said Nelson.

"Oh yes, lovely," agreed Mitzi.

"To fabulous new views and
horizons," declared Devon.

"Most definitely," added Cricket.

The bears applauded in the background. "This is the most special day ever!"

"I actually have gifts for all of us," announced Mitzi, trying hard to ignore the bears and their party dance. *"Earmuffs!"* Mitzi pulled out five pairs of homemade earmuffs,

perfectly sized for four adult
beavers and one baby beaver who
wanted to pretend that a group of
Super Happy Party Bears was not
dancing around them.

"Huzzah!" cheered the beavers,
and they clinked their glasses.

At that moment, a sound rose

122

up from the riverbank as the townscritters decided to add their own bit of flavor to the party. It was an ear-splitting combination of howling, yowling, and weepy screeching.

The townscritters gave it their all. But the beavers, under their earmuffs, didn't hear a thing.

CHAPTER NINE

The sun went down and the stars
came out. The townscritters kept
singing louder and louder and
louder, but it didn't do any good.
The beavers just relaxed in their
sunroom, enjoying the views that
only the best real estate along the
Grumpy River could provide.

Meanwhile, the bears cheered and chatted and cheered some more, never even caring that their new neighbors simply smiled politely and nodded gently so as to not disrupt the earmuffs atop their heads.

At one point, Mitzi drew the curtains, hoping not to even have to *look* at the bears partying on her lawn. But the bears simply exclaimed, "We LOVE shadow puppet shows!" and continued to party.

Gasping for breath and turning blue, the townscritters felt like failures once again.

"Maybe if Mayor Quill sings a solo . . ." suggested Sam.

The mayor's quills began to quake. A storm was brewing.

"No one needs to sing a solo, sir," Humphrey assured him. "I think if we sing for one more hour . . ." But glares from the other townscritters stopped Humphrey's thought.

"That's it!" fumed the mayor. "I'm putting an end to this. I will demand that they leave. After all, I am the MAYOR! It will be decreed!"

And he marched right up to the door of the lodge, but before he could knock—

"QUILLY!" cheered the bears. "You've come to the celebration!"

"This is no time to celebrate," said the mayor.

"Quilly, come dance with us!" begged the bears. They dragged Mayor Quill onto the dam and stuck a cup of juice in his hand. **"SHIMMY, SHIMMY, SHAKE!"** they chanted.

The dam shook. In fact, it shook
the earmuffs right off of Nelson's
head.

"This is an outrage!" said
Nelson, poking his head out of the
lodge. "Stop that this instant!"

But the bears continued to party.

Seeing how much the beavers were bothered by the dancing, the townscritters suddenly developed an interest in dancing, too.

"Oh, sir, those are some mighty fine dance moves," said Humphrey, joining in.

"I feel the beat in my feet!"
said Bernice as she stomped and
kicked her back feet. "Come on,
Dawn, let's clean up this dance
floor!"

In spite of themselves, the
residents of the Grumpy Woods
got their groove on.

The dam trembled. The logs quivered. The carefully constructed lodge started to creak.

"Nelson, do something!" shrieked Mitzi.

"I'm getting seasick," moaned Devon.

"It's a housewarming party!" cheered the bears. "Welcome home!"

Slide to the right.

Hop to the left.

Shimmy,
shimmy, shake.

Strike a pose.

By now the dam was really

hopping. Mayor Quill almost lost

his balance, and grabbed on to

Mops's tail for balance.

"CONGA LINE!" cheered Mops.

The conga line quickly formed

and made its way toward the shore,

with all the critters in tow. The

littlest bear brought up the rear, and as he jumped from the beaver dam to shore, his wee paw pushed off *just* enough to finally dislodge the whole wooden structure.

With a great shudder, the logs splintered and gave way. The dam broke as the Grumpy River came roaring through with a giant *whoosh*, and the lodge washed away with the current.

Nelson, Mitzi, Devon, Cricket, and the baby scrambled to the roof.

"If I'd wanted a yacht, I would have asked for a yacht!" screamed Mitzi.

Cricket pouted. "Next time we're hiring contractors."

Nelson and Devon put on their earmuffs. It was going to be a long ride downstream.

Back on shore, the bears waved good-bye to the beavers. "How clever of them to turn their house into a houseboat," said Shades.

"When living on a houseboat," stated Bubs, "the world is your backyard."

"BON VOYAGE! HAVE A GREAT CRUISE!" cheered the bears as they continued waving from the bank of the river. And you know what?

The townscritters cheered, too.

They were feeling just a *little* less grumpy. **THE END.**

A part of Macmillan Children's Publishing Group,
a division of Macmillan Publishing Group, LLC

SUPER HAPPY PARTY BEARS: KNOCK KNOCK ON WOOD.
Copyright © 2016 by Imprint. All rights reserved. Printed in China
by Toppan Leefung Printing Ltd., Dongguan City, Guangdong Province.
For information, address Imprint, 175 Fifth Avenue, New York, N.Y. 10010.

Library of Congress Cataloging-in-Publication Data is available.
ISBN 978-1-250-13117-1
Our books may be purchased in bulk for promotional, educational,
or business use. Please contact your local bookseller or the Macmillan
Corporate and Premium Sales Department at (800) 221-7945 ext. 5442
or by e-mail at MacmillanSpecialMarkets@macmillan.com.

Book design by Natalie C. Sousa
Imprint logo designed by Amanda Spielman
Illustrations by Steve James

First Edition—2016

1 3 5 7 9 10 8 6 4 2

mackids.com

If this book isn't yours, keep your thieving paws off it. Obey or may all of
your party horns fail to unroll, no matter how hard you blow.

TO BOWIE:
THANKS FOR THE INSPIRATION.

CHAPTER ONE

Welcome to the Grumpy Woods!

Well, not really. Just kidding.
You may as well just turn around
and go back. No one is welcome
here. The rock wall should have
made that clear.

It might not be a big wall, but it makes its point. You see, there used to be a tall wooden fence to keep out certain folks—especially bears. Especially bears who like to dance and sing and make doughnuts and have parties. But then a bunch of beavers chewed it down and used it for their dam. It's kind of a sore point around here.

In fact, there is a new Mayoral Decree regarding beavers. Let me see your teeth—you aren't a beaver, are you? Beavers are no longer welcome in the Grumpy Woods. But that is a different story from a different book.

Of course, right now you might be thinking, *Bears are cute* and *Parties are fun* and *What's so bad about beavers?* Cut it out. The animals of the Grumpy Woods do not agree, because every animal here is, well, *grumpy*.

That upturned log in the center of the woods is City Hall. No, it's not really a hall. It's often confused with other upturned logs in the Grumpy Woods, which really irks Mayor Quill. So he ordered a brand-new sign to officially mark It. He's really proud of that sign.

Well, Mayor Quill
held a very official
meeting at City Hall.
Everyone—from Opal Owl to Dawn
Fawn—attended.

At that particular meeting, it
was decided that new measures
must be taken to keep
strangers out of the
Grumpy Woods. No
one wanted to take
any chances after the
Beaver Incident.

So even though all welcome
signs, welcome mats, and
mailboxes had already been
removed, and the Welcome Wagon
had been rolled off the Grumpy
Cliff by an official decree of the
mayor, the townscritters decided
to take further
action to keep
the Grumpy
Woods free of
intruders.

Everyone voted. And that was that. It was very official.

Humphrey Hedgehog, assistant deputy to Mayor Quill, presented his blueprints for a new and improved Grumpy Fence. It wasn't so much a fence as a towering wall made of the heftiest rocks this side of the Grumpy River.

Construction started right away.

However, Bernice Bunny and Dawn Fawn struggled under the weight of the boulders.

After only five minutes on the job,
Opal Owl went on strike, claiming
she was molting from the stress of
carrying such heavy rocks.

And one of the largest stones got away from Squirrelly Sam and rolled onto Sherry Snake. It took the entire crew to free her.

When it was finished, it wasn't towering at all. It wasn't really even much of a wall. It was more like a pile. So Humphrey made everyone gather a bunch of twigs to stick along the top of it.

It isn't a very impressive "fence." But don't say that to Humphrey.

He does not want to admit the project was a disaster. He insists that Sherry still patrol along the fence twice a day.

And so, every day, everyone in the Grumpy Woods wakes up already needing a nap, takes a quick ride on a mood swing, and orders up some breakfast—two hot cross buns and a bowlful of *Who cares!*

That is, everyone except the
Super Happy Party Bears!
See the mailboxes dangling like
ornaments from the shrubbery?
And the welcome mats stacked like
a house of cards to create a cozy
canopy in front of
the main entrance?

That's the Party Patch, the

HEADQUARTERS OF FUN—

where the Super Happy Party Bears

have made their home. Life is very

different there. Life is super. Life is

happy. And life is full of parties!

If you follow the carefully placed

sticks, laid out in the shape of

arrows up the flower-lined path,
you'll see the welcome sign out
front. On top of the sign sits a little
stick-figure diorama that includes
the likeness of each Grumpy Woods
neighbor. They are wearing party
hats and dancing. The leader of the
party appears to be Mayor Quill.

See, while the others in the Grumpy Woods can't stand the bears, the Super Happy Party Bears *adore* their neighbors, especially the mayor.

And so, on a beautiful morning such as this, the Super Happy Party Bears get up at YAY O'CLOCK, take a quick walk on sunshine, and order up some breakfast—a bowlful of awesome sauce and a short stack of *Hot Diggity Dogs!*

Nothing annoys the critters of the Grumpy Woods more.

Except when the bears have a party.

And they are always having a party.

CHAPTER TWO

Knock knock, knockity knock.

All morning long, a rhythmic tapping had been shaking every leaf and disturbing every critter in the Grumpy Woods. Humphrey the Hedgehog was on an official mission to put an end to the racket.

He couldn't be happier. It was his longtime dream to evict the Super Happy Party Bears from the Grumpy Woods once and for all. Because whoever got rid of the

possible culprits

1. The Super EVICTED Party Bears

2. Thirsty Birds

Super Happy Party Bears would be a hero. And everyone knows that heroes can have statues of themselves in parks and have holidays on their birthdays and, most important, become mayors.

Mayor Quill was a fine mayor. But, truthfully, Humphrey thought the porcupine was a bit of a softie sometimes. He required evidence before tossing the bears out. Well, this time the evidence could be heard echoing off the trees. *Knock knock, knockity knock.*

Mayor Quill had declared by order of Mayoral Decree 427 that knocking was not permitted in the

Grumpy Woods. No one really visited anyone else anyway, so knocking on doors was no longer necessary. But it was up to Humphrey to find out who was to blame for the noise. Humphrey was pretty sure he knew where to start.

As he turned up the path to the Party Patch, lined with cheerful flowers and arrows made of twigs pointing toward the welcoming door, Humphrey stumbled over one of the twigs.

"Harrumph!" Humphrey kicked *all* the twigs, causing them to scatter. "Try following *that* path!" he muttered as he trudged on.

Once at the door, Humphrey banged loudly to be heard over the commotion inside. Official mayoral business allowed for the breaking of Mayoral Decree 427.

"You need to say 'Knock knock,'" instructed a voice on the other side of the door.

"Knock. Knock," he repeated.

"Who's there?" sang out the voice on the other side.

"Humphrey Hedgehog, assistant deputy to the mayor, His Excellency. I am on—"

"Humphrey *who*?" interrupted the melodic voice.

"OPEN THIS DOOR AT ONCE!" yelled Humphrey.

"You didn't say 'please,'" the voice sang out. This was true. And Humphrey didn't see the harm in being polite.

"*Please* open this door," said Humphrey.

The door swung wide open,
revealing a dance party of epic
proportions.

"HUMPHREY!" the bears all cheered.

And before he could object, Humphrey was pulled into the Party Patch, where a party hat was slapped on his spines and a cup of apple juice was put into his paw.

"I'm actually here on very important official business," said Humphrey, trying desperately to be heard over the music.

"What?" asked the bears. "We can't hear you." They continued to dance to the strong thumping bass.

"Very. Important. Official.

Business," yelled Humphrey.
"ABOUT THE MUSIC!"

"Isn't it FABULOUS?" asked
Shades, peering over his star
glasses.

"It's the best music ever!"
exclaimed Mops as he flipped his
mop-top hair to the beat.

Even the bubbles Bubs was calmly blowing in the corner seemed to bounce in rhythm. In fact, the entire Party Patch was shaking with the music.

Humphrey marched over to the Super Happy Party Band and

grabbed the microphone out of
Ziggy's paw, replacing it with his
own cup of juice.

"WE LOVE KARAOKE!"

cheered Ziggy.

"SUPER HAPPY KARAOKE TIME!
SUPER HAPPY
KARAOKE
TIME!" the
bears chanted,
and did their
Super Happy
Party Dance.

Slide to the right.

Hop to the left.

Shimmy, shimmy, shake.

Strike a pose.

One by one, Humphrey snatched
the instruments away from the
band—Jigs's maracas, Little Puff's
xylophone, and Flips's trumpet
(which was really just an inventive
way of using his party hat). Then,
with a spiny hip-check, he sent Big

Puff sliding across the dance floor, away from his pots-and-pans drum set and straight into a conga line.

Yet even without the Super Happy Party Band, the beat went on. But how?

Humphrey was flabbergasted.

Just then the littlest bear tugged on Humphrey's sleeve.

"Would you care to sing a duet?" said the littlest bear, looking at the microphone still in Humphrey's paw.

"What in the world is causing that horrendous knocking?" asked Humphrey, dropping all the instruments to cover his ears.

"Not *what* in the *world*," said
the littlest bear. "*Who* in the *trees*!"
And he pointed out the window to
a woodpecker pecking a beat into
every darn tree in the woods.

CHAPTER THREE

Humphrey stood at the bottom of a tree and looked up. Wallace Woodpecker was drumming with his beak, and by now it had given Humphrey a major headache.

"Excuse me," Humphrey called. "By order of the mayor, I am going to have to ask you to stop that noise this instant."

But Wallace could not hear Humphrey.

Small flakes of bark drifted to the ground like snowflakes as Wallace pecked on. A few chips fell onto Humphrey's nose, and he quickly *harrumphed* them off.

Using Flips's party hat as a
megaphone, Humphrey tried
once more. "You, in the tree!
I need to ask you to stop that.
Immediately!"

The drumming stopped.

"I think he has a song request,"
explained the littlest bear.

"Oh, okay. I thought maybe
I did something wrong," said
Wallace, and he flew down to take
Humphrey's request.

"Actually, I'm here on official
business," said Humphrey. "You
have to stop drumming. By order of
the mayor."

"What did I do
wrong?" asked Wallace.

"NOTHING!" cheered the bears. Humphrey scowled.

"I'll ask the questions here," said Humphrey. "Firstly, who are you?"

"Wallace Woodpecker," Wallace answered.

"He's our *new* friend!" the bears quickly added, and cheered.

Humphrey stayed focused on his

interrogation and made notes on
his clipboard. "Where did you come
from, Wallace? I've never seen you
around the Grumpy Woods before."

"Oh, I just got here!" said
Wallace. "They invited me." He
pointed to the bears, who beamed
proudly at their feathered buddy.

"We were out for a stroll this

morning when we heard the most
magnificent drumming," explained
Mops.

"It was perfect for sunrise
dancercising," added Jacks.

"So we invited Wallace to share
his most excellent skills with the

rest of the neighbors," continued Big Puff.

"In hopes that it would bring us all together," said the littlest bear sweetly.

"And it did! Humphrey's here!" the bears cheered.

"One last question: *How* did you get over the Grumpy Fence?" Humphrey was referring to his personal magnum opus, the newest

piece of architecture in the Grumpy

Woods, designed to keep out all

intruders. As mentioned in Chapter

One, it was really just a small pile of rocks and twigs.

Wallace simply fluttered his wings. "I flew!"

Humphrey growled. Obviously they needed a taller fence.

"Well, I am going to have to cite you for disrupting the peace in the Grumpy Woods," scolded Humphrey. "And you do not have a permit to perform music in public. So you must stop this instant."

"What is a permit?" asked Mops.

"If you have to ask, you don't
have one," snapped Humphrey.

"I'm so sorry," said Wallace,
hanging his head in shame. "I was
only trying to be a good neighbor."

"Good neighbors don't make
noise," whispered Humphrey.

The bears gathered around to comfort Wallace as Humphrey turned on his heel and left. Only one problem . . .

"How do you get out of this place?" Humphrey called back to the bears.

"Follow the twig arrows on the flower-lined path," they replied.

Humphrey looked down at the disheveled pile that *used* to be the twig arrows. How was he supposed to follow that? He spun around to complain, and his paw slipped on a loose twig.

Humphrey slid to the right. He hopped to the left. He wobbled on one foot, which caused him to shimmy and shake. And when he started to lose his balance, he quickly struck a pose. It all looked very familiar to the bears.

CHAPTER FOUR

"It's no use," sobbed Wallace as he flitted back up the trunk of the tree and gathered his belongings in his knapsack. "I'll never fit in anywhere!"

"Don't say that, Wallace," said the littlest bear. "You belong here with us."

"Birds of a feather stick together," proclaimed Bubs. He placed his party hat on his nose as if it were a beak. The bears *oooh*ed and slowly nodded in agreement.

"You don't understand," explained Wallace. "I've flown just about everywhere. But it's always the same. After a while, I am told

my pecking is too noisy and I'm kicked out. I'll never find a home."

"We LOVE your pecking!" cheered the bears.

"It makes me happy," added the littlest bear, giving his tush a little shake.

"But it made everyone else in the Grumpy Woods angry. I can't stay here now," said Wallace.

"Sure you can," said Big Puff. "All you have to do is show them hepcats there's more to you."

"There's nothing more to me," sobbed Wallace. "Nothing I do is good enough."

Just then, Flips looked at Wallace through his telescope (again, yet another use for his party hat) and spied something in the tree trunk behind him. Wallace's pecking had carved a beautiful design of swirls and curls into the bark.

"What is *that*?" asked Flips.

Wallace

blushed and tried   to hide

the handiwork with his wings. "It's

nothing. Just a little something I

do. It's doodles mostly. Nothing

special."

All the bears took turns viewing

the masterpiece through Flips's

telescope.

"IT'S BARK-TASTIC!"

they all agreed.

However, Wallace explained

that no one had a need for such

woodworking. He had been all over,

and no matter where he went, he

was told to leave the trees alone.

"Sounds like you've been pecking

up the *wrong* trees," said Mops.

"We have plenty of trees here

in the Grumpy Woods," said Little
Puff. "Well, we *did* have lots of
trees, before the beavers used
them to build their lodge. But more
are growing in."

"I'm not welcome here," said
Wallace. "You heard that angry
fellow with the spikes."

Wallace had a point. Humphrey had said that Wallace must stop drumming by order of the mayor. That sounded pretty official.

"Well, if you have to leave," said Ziggy, "let's at least play you some Super Happy exit music."

The Super Happy Party Band gathered their instruments from

the pile that Humphrey had dropped them in.

"One problem," said Jigs. "My maracas broke." She held up the sad pair of busted shakers.

"No worries," said Ziggy. "We can find a substitute."

"SEARCH PARTY!" cheered the bears as they looked for stand-in

maracas. They tested every
pinecone, leaf, and small stone, but
nothing seemed to work—until . . .

"Here ya go," said Wallace,
handing Jigs two perfectly whittled
wooden maracas. Little seeds
rattled inside. The handles had
been carved with care and a note
was attached to one of them.

Thanks for the friendship,
Neighbor.
Love, Wallace

"You made these?" asked Jigs, admiring Wallace's handiwork.

The woodpecker blushed. "Just a little something to remember me by." And he turned to leave.

"Wait!" said the bears. "You can't go!"

Wallace stopped, unsure of what the bears meant.

"Everyone needs a handyman to fix things up and make them beautiful," explained Mops. "Even in the Grumpy Woods!"

"Helping out is the perfect way to get neighbors to love you!" cheered the bears.

"Yeah. You can be our super

SUPER!"

said the littlest bear.

"Really? I can stay?" asked
Wallace as the bears all surrounded
him in a big bear hug. "HOORAY!
Wait. What's a super?"

CHAPTER FIVE

The bears explained that a super
was simply a supervisor who made
sure everything was shipshape
around the neighborhood and
that Wallace would be responsible
for repairs around the Grumpy
Woods. Wallace liked the sound

of that. After all, he just wanted
to make the other townscritters
happy.

So the bears all got right to
work transforming Wallace into the
super-est super the Grumpy Woods
could have. First, a tool belt,
a button-down
shirt that read
WALLY, and a set
of keys would help
Wallace look the
part. The keys

didn't actually open any doors in the Grumpy Woods. They were, in reality, just spoons. But the littlest bear insisted that the jingling noise was essential to the uniform.

Next, the bears provided Wallace with a map that showed every residence in the Grumpy Woods,

with each home clearly labeled.

That way, even those hidden *I want*

to be left alone homes—like Bernice

Bunny's—could be easily located.

And last, every handyman needs

a to-do list. So the bears wrote

down tasks for Wallace. Each task

was meant to fix and beautify the

Grumpy Woods, which would, in

theory, make every townscritter
fall in love with Wallace. Super
happily ever after.

"Here. In case you get hungry,"
said Shades, handing Wallace
a metal lunch box. "There are
doughnuts inside. There's even a
jelly one!"

With that, Wallace was off.

As he was finishing his first
job, high up in the trees, Wallace
noticed he wasn't alone. Someone
below was frantically humming her
favorite cleaning-up tune.

It was Dawn Fawn.

"Well, hello there," said Wallace,
flying down to introduce himself.
"I'm the new super of the Grumpy
Woods, and I—"

Dawn came in close. She
sniffed Wallace. She nudged his

key-spoons with her nose. She then
dusted his head off with her short
little tail.

"I need my dust bunny," she
squealed, and trotted off into the
brush.

"Cute. She wants to help," Wallace chuckled. But his chuckling was soon interrupted.

"WHOOOOOO are you?" said a pair of angry yellow eyes peeking out from the dense branches. It was Opal Owl, who was rarely seen in the Grumpy Woods. She liked it that way.

"Howdy-doody," said Wallace.
"I'm Wallace, the new super of the
Grumpy Woods, and I—"

"What did you dooOOOO to my
rooOOOOOof?"

"Oh that." Wallace blushed. "A
little handiwork is all, ma'am. No
need to pay
me. Just being
neighborly."

The yellow eyes only squinted
and waited for a better answer.

"It's a sunroof," said Wallace.
"The bears thought you might want
to let some light into your life."

"I'M NOCTURNAL!" screeched
Opal. "I like it dark."

"Maybe a moon-roof, then? I was only trying to help," said Wallace, hanging his head.

"WhoOOOOooo *asked* you toOOOOooo?" she screeched. Wallace was pretty sure her head spun completely around before he lost her in the bright sunlight.

Better luck with the next job,
thought Wallace, scanning his list.
Next stop was Bernice Bunny's
house and then on to City Hall.

CHAPTER SIX

At City Hall, Mayor Quill had just
sat down to nurse his headache
and have his midday bowl of
leaves and berries when someone
knocked on the door.

Knock knock.

"By order of Mayoral Decree four-two-seven—" declared Quill.

Bernice Bunny barged in, and she was hopping mad. **"MY BOOK HAS HOLES!"** she announced.

"I tried to stop her, sir," said Humphrey, who followed close behind. "I told her that *now* is no time for a book club meeting."

All day and night, Bernice Bunny's twitchy nose was stuck in a book—which meant the only time she stopped to say anything was

to either shush loud townscritters

or try to discuss her latest read.

So most of the Grumpy Woods
residents left her alone, not
wanting to engage in an unwanted
book club discussion.

"HOLES!" she declared once
again.

"So many books these days have
holes," dismissed Humphrey.

"Precisely," agreed Mayor Quill.

"There's a term for it. What are they called?"

"Plot holes, sir."

"Right, Humphrey. Plot holes."

"In fact," continued Quill, "it always bothered me that everything turns back to its original form at midnight *except* Cinderella's shoe. I mean, wouldn't that have disappeared or become some boring slipper or something?"

"Brilliant, sir," agreed Humphrey. "I never thought of that."

"No, no, NO!" yelled Bernice. "A real, live hole!" Bernice held up her book and then stuck her ear through the gaping hole and waved at Humphrey and Quill.

She went on to explain that every book in the south branch of her library—which is literally the southernmost branch in a low-lying bush, but don't tell her that—had been destroyed by similar holes.

"My dear Bernice," said the mayor, putting his prickly arm around her shoulders and guiding her slowly to the door, "book vandalism is quite a shame.

We will put it on the agenda for the next town meeting. Now, if you wouldn't mind . . . I am quite busy with *official* mayor business."

Squirrelly Sam, the Grumpy Woods' nosy forest gossip, suddenly appeared, scrambling down from the branches.

"Excuse me, Mr. Mayor.
You didn't hear this from me,
but someone seems to have
turned your City Hall sign into
Swiss cheese. There are holes
everywhere!"

Mayor Quill stomped his foot.
He shook from head to toe, and
just before he exploded, Humphrey
rolled into a defensive ball.

Quills shot out everywhere.
One narrowly missed Sam's tail.
Another soared straight through
the hole in Bernice's book.

Thankfully, she had already pulled her ear out of it.

Humphrey peeked from behind his clipboard.

"Hole in one, sir."

CHAPTER SEVEN

The sign that distinguished Mayor
Quill's City Hall from all the other
upturned logs in the area looked
like a grandma's doily collection.
The once-official-looking marker
was covered in swirly scrolls, and
several of the letters spelling out

CITY HALL were lost in an intricate
pattern. It was actually quite
elegant—unless you were grumpy.

"Preposterous!" proclaimed Quill.

"C-blank-blank-Y blank-A-L-blank," spelled Humphrey. "It looks like a puzzle on a game show."

"'COZY BALL'?" guessed Bernice.

"'CLAY WALK'?" guessed Humphrey.

"I'd like to buy a vowel," said Sam.

"NO ONE IS BUYING ANY VOWELS!" The spines on Mayor Quill's brow quivered, predicting

a storm. Just then, the ground
hissed.

"Newssss from the front linessss.
Ssssomeone needssss to buy a
new fence." It was Sherry Snake,
the self-proclaimed sheriff of the
Grumpy Woods.

"Why? What happened to my—

I mean, *our* fence, Sherry?" asked
Humphrey.

"Come on and ssssee for
yoursssselvessss," said Sherry.

The group paraded toward the
Grumpy Woods border, noticing
holes in every tree along the way.
It was as if they were in a life-sized

connect-the-dots game. And sure enough, the holes led them straight to the Grumpy Fence and the twigs on top.

"It looks polka-dotted," said Squirrelly Sam, sniffing at a larger hole in the twigs. He could see right through to the other side.

"I thought you were patrolling day and night, Sherry! How could this happen?" yelled Humphrey.

"That's *ssssheriff* to you, and yessss, I was patrolling. But thissss didn't happen on my watch! *Ssssomeone elsssse* was in charge!" She spit toward Sam.

"Me?" said Sam. "I told you I needed a break in the middle of the day for nut collecting and storage. I felt a chill in the air and I panicked, and I thought the winter was coming early and—"

"SILENCE!" said Quill. "This is vandalism! And vandalism such as this will not be tolerated in the Grumpy Woods!"

"Well said, sir. The culprit or *culprits* will be punished," said Humphrey.

"But who would do such a thing?" asked Bernice.

"Well, you didn't hear it from me," started Sam, "but everything is covered in holes. And what else has holes? Doughnuts. And who loves doughnuts?"

"The Ssssuper Happy Party Bearssss," answered Sherry.

Everyone gasped.

"Makes perfect sense," said Mayor Quill.

But before Mayor Quill could issue a warrant for the arrest of the Super Happy Party Bears, a frantic humming to a familiar cleaning-up tune came up along the wall toward the group. Dawn Fawn was feverishly sweeping up dust. It seemed that whoever had drilled all those holes into the Grumpy Fence had caused quite a mess.

"Dirty bird! Dirty bird! Dirty bird!"

Dawn sang on repeat.

Then
Dawn caught
a glimpse of
Bernice and
shrieked, "I
NEED MY DUST
BUNNY!" Before
Bernice could

103

react, Dawn scooped up the bunny
with her mouth and started using
Bernice's cottontail to tidy up the
hills of dust.

"*Eeek!*" screamed Bernice. "Help
me!"

"Whatever is going on here?"
asked Mayor Quill. "Who is this
'dirty bird' you sing of?"

Dawn's simple description of a woodpecker was enough for Humphrey to know *exactly* who was to blame.

"I'll call a town meeting," said Humphrey.

"Sssshall I go make an arresssst?" asked Sheriff Sherry.

"Knock yourself out," said Quill.

CHAPTER EIGHT

Wallace Woodpecker was very
tired by the time he returned
to the Party Patch. His eyelids
drooped, and he was dragging his
wings. The bears were eager to
find out how his day had gone.

Wallace dropped his lunch box at the door and sighed.

"Well?" asked Mops.

"How was it being the super today?" asked Shades.

"I don't know," said Wallace. "I'm not sure they will like what I did."

"What do you mean?" asked Jigs.

"Of course they will!" She gave her maracas an enthusiastic shake.

"I can almost hear the love now," said the littlest bear.

The littlest bear was right. There was some sort of noise in the distance, but it wasn't love. It was a mob of angry critters, and it was marching straight up the flower-lined path.

All the Grumpy Woods townscritters soon arrived on

the bears' doorstep, even Opal
Owl, who was, of course, wide
awake and had spotted the pack
as they passed her tree. She gladly
abandoned her jigsaw puzzle, put
on her darkest
sunglasses, and
tagged along.

"Come out with your pawssss up!" instructed Sheriff Sherry, now taking on a very official role.

The bears thought Sherry just wanted them all to *wave their paws in the air like they just don't care* and got very excited.

"See, Wally! They love you!" cheered the bears. And they all burst out the door to join the We Love Wallace celebration. "IT'S SUPER HAPPY PARTY TIME! SUPER HAPPY PARTY TIME!"

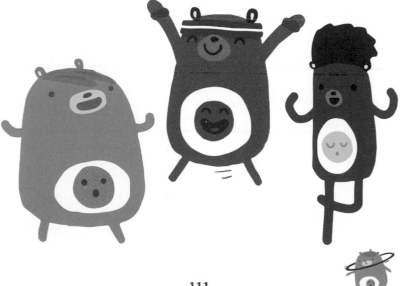

Slide to the right.

Hop to the left.

Shimmy, shimmy, shake.

Strike a pose.

"Where's Wallace Woodpecker?" asked Humphrey.

"Wallace!" the bears called into the Party Patch. "Your fans are looking for you!"

Wallace bashfully stepped outside.

"You ruined my tree AND my sleep!" screeched Opal Owl.

"I said I was sorry," replied
Wallace.

"You made holes in all of my
books!" accused Bernice Bunny.

"I was exterminating the
bookworms," explained Wallace.

"You made a mockery of City
Hall!" yelled Mayor Quill.

"I was decorating and got carried away," said Wallace, holding back tears. "I thought maybe a nice pattern would look very classy and official!"

"YOU DESTROYED MY GRUMPY FENCE!" screamed Humphrey.

Everyone froze, then looked at Humphrey.

"*OUR* GRUMPY FENCE!" Humphrey corrected himself.

"I made it so Sherry could see through it, and patrol on *both* sides of the wall at once," Wallace said, and burst into tears. "It's no use. I'm not super. I'm a failure!"

Wallace took off his tool belt and his jingly spoons and flew up into the tree.

"Come down here this instant," said Mayor Quill. "We're not through with you!"

Wallace flew even higher, bumping into one of the Super

Happy Party Bears' mailboxes,
which fell to the ground with a
bang. Out spilled one envelope.

"WE'VE GOT MAIL!" cheered the
bears.

"It's from the beavers!" said the
littlest bear as he tore it open.

"Ooh! Is it a
postcard from
their cruise?"
asked Mops.

"What's this word here? 'Suing'?" asked the littlest bear.

"It's supposed to be 'seeing.' It's a typo," explained Bubs as he blew bubbles in the corner. "It says they will be *seeing* us."

Dear Super Happy Annoying Bears,

We will be suing you.

Truly,
The Beavers

The Bears
Party Patch
Grumpy Woods

"Here's a photograph of their houseboat," said the littlest bear as he passed it around.

Everyone admired the houseboat—even the townscritters.

"It's a little plain, though," said Jigs. "I bet Wallace could do some fine woodworking for them."

"THAT'S IT!" cheered the bears.

"The beavers LOVE fine art and furnishings," said Mops. "Wallace could do woodworking for the beavers!"

Wallace drifted back down to the ground. "You think they would like my work?"

Mayor Quill immediately joined in. "Of course, Wallace. Opportunity knocks! Answer that door!"

The other townscritters caught on quickly. They were very eager to send Wallace off on this adventure, so they changed their tune and started handing out compliments.

"Have yoooou seen the be-yoooo-tiful sunroooof Wallace made me?" Opal Owl asked the others. "It's cured my daytime drowsiness."

Everyone applauded.

"Wallace got rid of every bookworm in my library while also getting rid of all the boring parts in my books," boasted Bernice.

Humphrey patted Wallace on the back.

"And the City Hall sign!" added Mayor Quill. "Not only is it super fancy, but the misplaced letters also add a layer of mystery to the place."

"Thank you," said Wallace. "I don't know what to say. I really appreciate your belief in me."

Mayor Quill placed his prickly arm around Wallace's shoulders and guided him toward the

flower-lined path. "So I guess this is good-bye, then, Wallace."

"Wait!" said the littlest bear. "Aren't you forgetting something?"

"It's time for a SUPER HAPPY GOING-AWAY PARTY!" cheered the bears.

CHAPTER NINE

The bears threw a Going-Away
Party fit for the super-est of supers,
complete with doughnuts and
dancercise. All the townscritters
were there. They were so pleased
that the noise was going to stop
that they even partied a
little bit themselves.

Ziggy played guitar. Well, it wasn't really a guitar. More like a few rubber bands stretched across a beautifully carved piece of wood—courtesy of Wallace.

The Super Happy Party Band played their signature dance remix of "If You're Happy and You Know It." Dawn Fawn even joined in and sang a few bars.

Sherry Snake and Flips started
a rousing game of doughnut
ringtoss. Sherry didn't mind having
doughnuts tossed at her. She loved
sinking her teeth into each one that
found its way around her neck.

And Humphrey shared stories
of his life in City Hall. Actually,
Bubs was the only one listening. He
calmly blew his party bubbles as
Humphrey went on and on.

It was a good time for all. But

soon it was time for good-bye and
to send Wallace off in search of an
exciting career as a woodworker.

All the bears gave Wallace a
hug. The woodpecker spread his
wings out and said, "Thank you

all so much! You have helped me
find what I was meant to do! You
are my best friends!" Then Wallace
grabbed his knapsack and headed
down the flower-lined path.

"Send us a postcard," said the
littlest bear.

"IT'S SUPER SUPER WALLY TIME! SUPER SUPER WALLY TIME!" cheered the bears, and they did their Super Happy Party Dance. And you know what?

The townscritters danced, too.

They were feeling just a *little less grumpy*. THE END.

ABOUT THE AUTHOR

In previous chapters, Marcie Colleen has been a teacher, an actress, and a nanny, but now she spends her days writing children's books! She lives in her very own Party Patch, Headquarters of Fun, with her husband and their mischievous sock monkey in San Diego, California. Occasionally, there are even doughnuts. This is her first chapter book series.